EARLY BIRD STORIES™

MW00887189

Jada Sticks with It
A Story about Determination

Mari Schuh   Illustrated by Mike Byrne

LERNER PUBLICATIONS ◆ MINNEAPOLIS

NOTE TO EDUCATORS

Find text recall questions at the end of each chapter. Critical-thinking and text feature questions are available on page 23. These help young readers learn to think critically about the topic by using the text, text features, and illustrations.

Lerner Publications Company
An imprint of Lerner Publishing Group, Inc.
241 First Avenue North
Minneapolis, MN 55401 USA

For reading levels and more information, look up this title at www.lernerbooks.com.

Main body text set in Billy Infant.
Typeface provided by SparkyType.

Photos on p. 22 used with permission of: Digital Media Pro/Shutterstock (baseball); Rawpixel.com/Shutterstock (trophy).

Library of Congress Cataloging-in-Publication Data

Names: Schuh, Mari C., 1975- author. | Byrne, Mike, 1979- illustrator.
Title: Jada sticks with it : a story about determination / Mari Schuh ; illustrated by Mike Byrne.
Description: Minneapolis : Lerner Publications, [2023] | Series: Building character (Early bird stories) | Includes bibliographical references and index. | Audience: Ages 4-9. | Audience: Grades 2-3. | Summary: "Jada is working on a big science project, but distractions seem to be everywhere! Jada sticks with it and learns that a little determination goes a long way"— Provided by publisher.
Identifiers: LCCN 2022010109 (print) | LCCN 2022010110 (ebook) | ISBN 9781728476391 (library binding) | ISBN 9781728478432 (paperback) | ISBN 9781728481630 (ebook)
Subjects: CYAC: Determination (Personality trait)—Fiction. | Conduct of life—Fiction. | LCGFT: Picture books.
Classification: LCC PZ7.1.S33655 Jad 2023 (print) | LCC PZ7.1.S33655 (ebook) | DDC [E]—dc23

LC record available at https://lccn.loc.gov/2022010109
LC ebook record available at https://lccn.loc.gov/2022010110

Manufactured in the United States of America
3-1010766-50660-3/11/2024

TABLE OF CONTENTS

CHAPTER 1

A BIG PROJECT

Bzzzz! Dad's phone buzzes.

"Your cousin Lisa texted," Dad says.

"Jada, do you want to text her back?"

Lisa is one of my favorite people. But I need to focus.

"I'm working on my science project," I say. "Tell Lisa I'll text later!"

I'm testing whether plants grow best in water, milk, juice, or soda.

I pour a liquid on each of my plants.

I measure how much the plants have grown. In my science notebook, I record what I find.

It hasn't always been easy. But I keep at it no matter what!

Ding-dong! The doorbell rings. Who could it be?

Check! What is Jada testing in her project?

CHAPTER 2

STAYING FOCUSED

"Jada, it's your friends!" Mom says.

"Can you play?" Diego asks.

"Not today," I say. "I want to, but I'm working on my project."

"Let's play tomorrow!" I add.

"OK!" Sara answers.

"Are you ready to get back to your project?" Mom asks.

"For sure!" I reply.

Check! Why does Jada say she can't play?

CHAPTER 3

NEVER GIVING UP

I plan to finish my project today, but . . .

"No, kitty," I say. "Don't play with the plants!"

"Joey, watch out! You'll break the pot!"

"I want orange juice!" says my sister.

"Oh no! That's for my project," I tell her.

Dad starts getting dinner ready. He moves my things.

"But the plants won't get sun if they aren't by a window!" I say. "I'll move them to my bedroom window."

Check!
What does Jada's sister want?

See my chart? The plant that grew in water grew the best!

I did it! I'm done with my project.

I give it to my teacher.

"How did it go?" she asks.

"Perfect!" I say. "Just perfect."

Check! Which plant grew the best?

21

LEARN ABOUT DETERMINATION

Determination means not giving up.

Determined people believe in themselves.

Determination is also called grit.

Determined people keep their eyes on the prize!

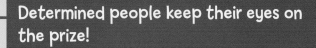

Determined people find creative ways to get things done.

THINK ABOUT DETERMINATION:
CRITICAL-THINKING AND TEXT FEATURE QUESTIONS

When was a time you had determination?

Who is this book's author?

What is your biggest goal?

What page does chapter 4 start on?

GLOSSARY

chart: a way of presenting data in a simple form, also called a graph

focus: to give something attention

liquid: a wet substance that you can pour

project: an assignment worked on over a period of time

LEARN MORE

KidsHealth: Feelings
https://kidshealth.org/en/kids/feeling/

Krekelberg, Alyssa. *Stop and Think: Learning about Self-Discipline.* Mankato, MN: Child's World, 2020.

Schuh, Mari. *Luis's First Day: A Story about Courage.* Minneapolis: Lerner Publications, 2023.

INDEX